GOLEM
GOES TO
CAMP

By Todd Gutnick
Illustrated by Ruth Bennett

APPLES & HONEY PRESS

To my campers, fondly remembered,
and to campers everywhere
— TG

For Mary, Richard, and Celia
— RB

Apples & Honey Press
An Imprint of Behrman House Publishers
Millburn, New Jersey 07041
www.applesandhoneypress.com

ISBN 978-1-68115-622-4

Library of Congress Catalog Number: 2022946508

Design by David Neuhaus/NeuStudio
Edited by Dena Neusner
Printed in the United States of America

1 3 5 7 9 8 6 4 2

CONTENTS

CONTENTS

CHAPTER 1

COHENS TO CAMP

I swear I didn't mean for it to happen. No one believes me. And yet I really, truly, honestly never meant it to happen.

This is the story of my summer. The summer I turned ten. The summer I lost my first molar. The summer I learned to shoot a bow and arrow straight and improved my backstroke.

The summer I turned an ordinary pile

of mud into a powerful, moving thing.

I call it a "thing" because even though it had legs and arms, it wasn't alive. It couldn't breathe. It couldn't think. It didn't speak or have a family or even a pet. It could listen to simple instructions and follow them. But it had no feelings or favorite sports teams. It was a great big hunk of mud.

Well . . . it was more than just a lump of mud. It was a golem.

You've never heard of a golem? I'm not surprised. What kid has heard of a golem? I hadn't either before this summer.

But wait, I'm getting ahead of myself.

My name is Emmett. That may be the single most important fact of this story. You'll find out why soon enough.

Most of the time I live in Philadelphia with my younger sister, Emily, and my dog, Silo. But this summer Emily and I spent seven weeks at Camp Teva, in upstate New York, near the Catskill Mountains. It was my second year at camp—but boy, it felt totally different this year.

For one thing, I decided to take art, which normally I would never do.

And then there was the golem.

The second couldn't have happened without the first.

Do your parents ever try to push you to do something that you don't really want to do? That summer, my parents were really pushing.

My mom and dad are "creative types." I mean, that's what *they* call themselves anyway. My mom, Candy Cohen, is a writer for a magazine, and my dad is a painter and sculptor, the sorta famous artist Peter Cohen. You've heard of him? Maybe not.

But I'm not that big on art. I'm

into skateboards, comic books, and computers—those kinds of things. But drawing and painting? Not so much.

It's hard being a kid with a dad who is super-talented and famous. People expect things of you. My art teacher at school always made a big deal about it, and it was just *soooo* embarrassing.

Camp Teva offers a bunch of fun activities—nature hikes, canoeing, tennis, baseball, basketball, woodworking, archery, gaga, and lots more. And art, like everything else—except swimming lessons—is "an elective," a fancy word for something you don't have to do unless you want to.

I didn't want to, but my mom was insistent.

"Ugh. Whyyyyy?" I whined on the long drive to camp.

"Because we'd like you to try something

new this year," my mom said, gripping the steering wheel of our minivan. "Hey, you have a creative spirit, Em. You really do. Your sister is going to try tennis this summer, so why not try something outside your comfort zone?"

"Mom! You *know* I'm not good at art," I complained. "I can't even draw a rainbow. My lines are always squiggly. Emily says my people look like sticks. Don't you, Em?" My younger sister has real artistic talent. She is nine but had spent an entire year creating a book of pencil drawings.

"Mm-hmm," hummed Emily, who was

not paying attention, her face buried in her phone.

There was a long pause as I stared out the window, the trees whizzing by in a blur. The highway had shifted from four lanes to two, the scenery from buildings and billboards to green hills, cow pastures, and forests.

Mom made eye contact with me in the rearview mirror. "Emmett, it's just one week of art out of seven weeks at camp. Miss Rachel is an amazing teacher. Besides, your father will be thrilled you tried something close to his heart!" She patted my dad's leg in the passenger seat.

Dad's response was a loud snore. He was fast asleep. I turned back to my *Incredible Hulk* comic book.

Soon I felt the crunch of gravel under our wheels as we made the last turn into the camp gates. Trees shaded the long driveway up the hill into a clearing, where we were greeted by cheering groups of counselors holding "Shalom" and "Welcome Back!" signs and banging tambourines.

The Beetle ran up to our car and gave us both high fives as we piled out.

Who, or what, is "the Beetle," you ask? That's Mr. Beetleman, the camp director. His face is sorta beetle-like, and sometimes he scrunches up his eyes and wrinkles his forehead when he can't figure something out. I can't remember who came up with that nickname for him, but it stuck.

"Hey, it's the two Ems—Emmett and Emily! Welcome back Cohens. We missed you! Okay. First things first: turn off those screens; it's back-to-nature time."

Like nearly every other overnight camp in the wilderness, ours has a strict "no tech" policy. All campers' phones are turned in to the office when you arrive. No exceptions.

I powered down my phone and handed it to the Beetle. My phone-addicted sister was still staring at her glowing screen, and I giggled as Dad finally had to pry it from her hands while Emily whined about not being able to send a last text to a friend.

Mr. Beetleman handed us name tags and asked us to write our names in both Hebrew and English. I had already learned how to write my Hebrew name, but Emily, being younger, needed some help.

I hugged my parents one last time and then found my way to the ten-year-old boys' cabins near the woods.

My first day at the art shed was beautiful—sunny and clear, the perfect day for playing kickball or swimming in the lake. But not me. I was stuck indoors, being asked to choose between acrylic paint, watercolors, macramé, or clay. I was all squirmy, wearing a heavy, scratchy denim smock over my bathing suit and tank top.

I had had a rough night. I was a little homesick and missing Mom and Dad and Silo, my labradoodle.

Add to that the teasing of the twins, and I was about to burst.

Lilly and Rebecca were Emily's nine-year-old camp friends. You could always see them coming a mile away because of their bright, color-coordinated outfits.

The twins had heard how unhappy I was about taking art—and had been rubbing it in all day.

"Ooohh, Emmett. What're you gonna make?" Lilly cooed.

Rebecca chimed in before I could reply. "A painting of . . . pretty flowers?"

"A pretty pink and green bracelet for your girrlllfrriend?" Lilly slurred, to be extra annoying. More giggles.

Rebecca and Lilly whispered to each other, then purred together: "A uuuunnicorn?"

I pretended they weren't there and started poking around the shed for a project. In the back was a metal trash can, lined with a clear plastic bag. And inside was . . . boom! Just what I was looking for.

Mud! Thick, glorious, slimy mud. It was perfect! Pretty much the opposite of "pretty." Instead of making art, I would build an ugly mud monster (Emmett 1, parents 0).

The claylike mud was grayish brown and smelled faintly like the masks my mom sometimes rubs on her face at night. It shimmered in my hands and oozed through the spaces between my fingers.

Parking myself at a back table, I began shaping the clay, dipping my fingertips into water to work the mud and make it smooth. I'm telling you, the thing almost formed itself. By the end of the first half hour, I'd built the top half of a mini-monster, complete with arms and a large blocklike head.

I stood back and admired my work.

Then along came the critics.

"What is thaaat?" cried Lilly, scrunching up her face like she'd just been asked to eat brussels sprouts.

"Ugh, that's hideous! A mud creature? *Of course* a mud creature," added Rebecca. "What else?"

I got very annoyed at that point, so I went back to the trash can and grabbed another huge armful of mud. Then I tuned out the voices and imagined myself in an operating room like Dr. Frankenstein. There on the table I rolled out two thick trunks for legs.

Miss Rachel, the art counselor, stopped

by as I was slapping down even larger slabs of mud to fill out the monster's chest. "Hmm. Now this is . . . interesting," she said, pausing at my worktable and trying to find some kind words to say. "What is it meant to be?"

"I dunno," I responded, smiling to myself. "I just wanted to make something large with clay."

I actually had no idea what had gotten into my head. Had I devoured too many *Incredible Hulk* comics before camp? Maybe.

But whatever. Soon it was finished. With all the mud I added, my creature was now nearly as big as me. There it was, staring back at me with hollow little eyes, small thin lips, a hint of a nose with circular nostrils, its thick neck supporting a blocky head. Attached to its large chest were two stumpy arms and legs.

"It's awfully large," Miss Rachel said. "Where did you find this mud? This isn't what we normally use for pottery."

"It was in that large silver can in the back," I said, pointing to the supplies.

"Oh, wait! That's a special mixture of mud from the Dead Sea in Israel and hard clay I got from an artist friend in Prague. You weren't supposed to use it for projects. Didn't you see the 'Keep Out' sign on the top of the bin?"

Nope. I hadn't seen the sign. How was I supposed to know that this was special mud? And whoever heard of mud being special anyway?

I looked back at my creation. It was beginning to harden.

"Well, our time today is nearly up, so you'll need to put your name on it and store it next to the drying shelves over there." She pointed to a set of wooden shelves along the far wall. "Tonight I'll fire it in the kiln."

She handed me a small pointy stick. There wasn't enough room to spell out my full name on its forehead, so I carved the letters of my Hebrew name instead. In Hebrew, spelling *Emmett* takes only three letters—*alef, mem, ta*v. This is what they look like:

$$\text{א מ ת}$$

I gently picked up the creature and stood it on the floor. The thingy was almost as tall as four-foot-six me and felt like it weighed a ton. I propped it against the wall next to the shelves where other mud and clay projects were drying.

Flinging off the denim smock, I washed the mud off my hands at the slop sink and grabbed my swim bag.

"Bye, Emmett," Miss Rachel called from the back. "See you tomorrow."

I smiled and turned to wave. Arts and crafts hadn't been so terrible after all. As I raced out the door, I glanced back to where the mud creature was drying.

Its mouth was curved upward, almost like a smile.

Hmm, I don't remember giving it a smile, I thought as I headed off to the lake.

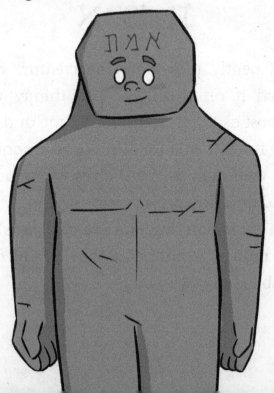

CHAPTER 2

ART APPRECIATION

The week passed quickly in a series of mornings filled with paint, papier-mâché, popsicle sticks, and colored pipe cleaners. Before I knew it, it was almost the weekend. "I think I'm done with art," I told my camp best friend and bunkmate, Jake, as we returned from morning activities to our bunk that Friday.

Jake frowned at my growing art collection—the pictures, pipe cleaners, and popsicle-stick mobiles now decorating the wall shelf next to my bunk. I had plunked the mud statue in a corner of the cabin we shared with the other boys in our group. It was the only place it would fit.

After a week of camp, our bunk was already starting to feel lived in. There were piles of dirty clothes, games, and books flung around on the floor, wet bathing suits under beds, sand tracked in from the lake,

dirt from the woods. The counselors were getting on our case. So the mud creature in the corner kinda blended right in.

"Now *THIS* is GREAT ART!" Jake said, walking by the creature slowly and cupping his chin in his hand like some goofy people do at art museums. We both laughed.

Jake Wiseman and I had bonded at camp last summer. I knew we'd be fast friends when he opened his trunk to reveal an entire collection of prank toys— whoopee cushions, piles of fake dog poop, plastic spiders, those things that wind up and give someone a shock when you shake their hand, and other cool stuff. Boy, did we have fun with those!

When I arrived this year, Jake had already saved me the lower bunk beneath his.

Jake was no longer the puny kid I

remembered from a year ago. Winter had passed—he in New York City, me in Philadelphia—and he was now a full size larger than me. His curly brown hair was the same as ever, though. And he still had the same silly grin and trunk full of prank toys and trick cards.

I was smaller than most of the boys in my unit. I wasn't the tallest or the fastest. But it didn't matter. Jake and I were still best buds.

Now we had something new to laugh about—the mud creature who'd taken over one corner of our cabin.

Jake inspected it closely. "Man, what were you THINKING? That thing is freakish."

The other boys in our bunk were getting ready for lunch, talking loudly, changing out of swimsuits, and slamming their trunk lids. A few others came over and gawked at my statue.

"Guys," our counselor Benjy's voice boomed from outside. "Line up! It's time for lunch."

"Ugh, am I going to have to look at that thing every day?" said Rob, a baseball fanatic who was the fastest kid in our unit. "I can't live with that thing staring at me when I'm getting undressed."

"Reminds me of the Ultimate Clayface out of DC Comics," said Danny, a new kid this summer. "Out of DC. Out of DC Comics. Like Clayface," Danny repeated.

Danny has autism spectrum disorder. People call it autism for short. That means his brain works differently than in kids without autism. Sometimes Danny repeats his words a couple of times. Sometimes he waves his hands or jumps up and down, especially when he's excited. And . . . he knows absolutely everything about comic books. After a week at camp,

I was already getting used to him. But not everyone had gotten the memo.

"Okay, okay, Danny, we get it," Rob rudely interrupted.

I jumped in. "It's no big deal, he's just saying the words again. Give him a break."

Rob backed off. "Oh, right. Sorry, Danny."

"Well, Clayface or not, I'm with you, Rob. This thing has got to go," Jake said. "I say we put it in one of the counselor's beds and give 'em a nice surprise tonight at bedtime." More laughs.

"The problem with you is you just don't appreciate fine art," I joked, pushing my nose up and squinting my eyes. Everyone laughed. "Come on, you have to admit it's pretty cool. I'm kinda proud of it myself."

"But what are you gonna do with it . . . do with it?" Danny asked. "You can't take it home with you—it's too big to fit in the car. And you can't leave it standing in here all summer. It's really gross and it *smells*."

"Guys!" Benjy's suntanned face popped into the doorframe. "Line up outside, please! Let's go! We don't have all day. You don't want the ten-year-old girls getting there first and eating all the food, do ya?"

Benjy is a fun counselor, but he's super competitive. He turns everything into a race, even something as basic as getting lunch. My bunkmates sprinted out the door. I went back to my bunk to grab my Crocs.

Jake was still inside the cabin. He was standing in front of the mud creature, frozen in place, the color drained from his face. "What the . . .?" His voice trailed off.

"What is it?" I asked.

Jake pointed at the back corner. "Either I'm losing it, or this thing just winked at me."

I peered into the monster's muddy face. Its eyes were wide and round, just as I'd made them.

"Dude, you're seeing things. Maybe you've had too much sun. C'mon." I grabbed his arm to head for the door.

Just then, slowly, the mud creature's left eye winked shut, and its clay lips curved up into a waxy smile.

Too stunned to speak, Jake and I sprinted out of the cabin.

CHAPTER 3

WHO'S PRANKING US?

"Hey guys, what's the matter? You've barely eaten anything." Benjy was staring at us behind his lunch tray, his fork hovering in midair.

"Just not hungry," I muttered.

"I'm starving, actually. Just not loving this food," said Jake.

I squinted in the bright sunlight of the dining hall. The room echoed with the excited energy of more than a hundred kids at summer camp.

I had barely touched my food, even though it was my favorite: chicken tenders and applesauce.

"What happened back there?" Jake whispered next to me.

"I dunno. That was crazy."

"Okay, you're playing a trick on me, right? What's inside that thing?"

"Huh? Nothing," I said quietly. "It's just a hunk of clay."

"But what did you put in its face to make it move? Did you bring a robotics kit from home or something?" I shook my head. "Are there batteries inside?" I shook my head again.

"You think one of the counselors is pranking us?"

I thought for a second. "Nah, I just brought it back from the art shed. No one's touched it."

"Well, you should destroy it as soon as we get back. Like, hack it into a thousand pieces. I didn't plan on sharing my bunk this summer with Swampman. And I'm *not* going to be its first victim."

"Definitely," I half agreed, picking at my food.

"But why would it wink and smile at us?" Jake asked. "And *after* everyone else left. Like it was trying to send a signal or something."

I shrugged.

"Think back to when you made it. Did you add anything besides mud?" Jake asked.

"No, I just took a hunk of mud and shaped it."

Jake thought some more, then shrugged. "It's a mystery, this monster of yours."

"What monster?" came a voice from right behind us.

I was so distracted I hadn't noticed Reisha sitting at the table behind us.

Reisha was ten, like us. She was the smartest kid in her grade but would never admit it to anyone. She was like a walking dictionary on two legs.

Jake and I moved ourselves and our trays over to Reisha's table. She was sitting by herself and holding a small book.

"Why were you two just whispering about a monster?"

"Something's up and we need your help," said Jake.

"Okay, shoot."

I told her the story of my project. How I had used the special mud with the "Keep Out" label on the can and had made it as tall as myself. How I had given it a head and a body and legs and arms and written my name on the forehead. How Miss Rachel had fired it in the kiln and then I brought it to our cabin. And how it had just now smiled and winked at us.

Reisha's hazel eyes grew rounder and rounder behind her thick glasses. Then a frown formed around the edges of her mouth.

"You guys really think I'd fall for that one? *'Guess what? I*

made a golem in art class.' Right! I'm not that gullible."

"Huh?" I shrunk back. Sometimes she talked like a dictionary too.

"*Gullible*, you know. Easily tricked. Well, nice try, Emmett and Jake. Everyone knows that old golem nonsense isn't real. It's the stuff of Jewish fairy tales. Now leave me alone—I'm helping lead Shabbat services tonight, and I have to finish reviewing this." She went back to studying the pages of what I now noticed was a small prayer book.

There was that word again: golem.

"What'd you say?" I asked. "What the heck is a golem?"

Just at that moment along came the twins, passing our table in bright-purple matching dresses, trays loaded with food. "Hey Emmett, how's mister muh-muh-mud monster?" teased Rebecca.

"Are you taking your 'muddy buddy' to Shabbat services tonight?" added Lilly. "Maybe it can lead!" Giggles as they walked away.

Reisha stared at us. "Wait! You two are serious, aren't you?"

"Deadly serious," answered Jake. "Umm, Reisha, you didn't answer Emmett's question. What's a go-lem?"

"Guys, I'll explain later. Meet me in the woods behind your cabin in one hour. Tell no one where you're going. And bring your new *friend*," she emphasized, meaning my monster.

CHAPTER 4

A PUFF OF AIR

Reisha was sitting on a stump in the woods when Jake and I showed up with our "new friend," which we'd wrapped in a white bedsheet. The shock of seeing it smile still hadn't worn off—even though the smile had vanished—and I wasn't ready to carry something with my bare hands that might, at any moment, start to wriggle and squirm.

As I got closer, I was annoyed to see

someone else sitting next to Reisha. It was Emily, my little sister, who adored Reisha and trailed her everywhere—the big sister she desperately wanted but never had.

I set the mud figure down next to the tree stump and unwrapped the sheet. Reisha's eyes grew wide, and my sister gasped.

Reisha nodded her head slowly, her thick curls bobbing.

"Oh wow," she said. "I didn't think it would be this big. Wait, you wrote Emmett on its forehead? *Emmett!* Seriously, are you messing with me? It's a golem!"

There was that word again. I shrugged. "Emmett's my name—what's the big deal? Kids put their names on art projects all the time."

"Wait. Don't you know? I mean, you're Jewish and all. And you never heard of a golem? Think for a minute: Prague, sixteenth century. Kabbalah? Does any of this ring a bell?"

"Umm, nope." I looked over at Jake. He was shaking his head too.

"Okay, boys, sit down. It's story time!"

Reisha pushed her glasses into place, cleared her throat, and began:

"In the sixteenth century, the Jews living in the old city of Prague weren't treated very well. They were forced to live separately from the rest of the people, in a section of the city called a ghetto. Crowds would tease and taunt them, or steal from them, or do much, much worse."

Reisha paused to make sure we were still with her.

"The chief rabbi of Prague, who had studied ancient teachings called Kabbalah, wanted to protect his people. So he used his mystical powers to create a golem. Now, the word *golem*, that comes from Hebrew. It means 'lump.' Like a lump of clay."

I nodded and glanced over at my project. Jake's face was turning bright pink. "Wait a minute. Emmett, didn't you say the special mud in the 'Keep Out' bucket was *from Prague*?"

"Umm, yeah. And also mud from the Dead Sea." I was getting weirded out big-time.

Reisha continued, "And you know the story of Adam and Eve, right?"

"Of course. Everybody knows *that*," I said, with a roll of my eyes.

"Well," she went on, "in ancient times it was said that when Adam was created, he was unfinished and a *golem*, only a lump of earth—until God gave him a soul."

"What's that got to do with the rabbi in Prague?" I asked.

"Well, legend has it this rabbi created his golem out of mud from the riverbed. He made the massive creature come to life—and it came to the Jewish people's rescue again and again, using its power to fight evil."

"Then what happened?" asked Jake.

"I don't exactly remember, but I think the story ends when the rabbi kills the golem and stores it in the attic of the Prague synagogue to keep it from making more mistakes."

I thought a minute. "Mistakes! What mistakes?"

"Since the golem didn't have a brain, you can imagine there were some pretty big mess-ups."

I looked at my creation. "You think I created a *golem*? How's that possible? I'm not a rabbi. I don't have mystical powers. I haven't even had a bar mitzvah yet."

"And the story's not real, right?" chimed in Emily, twirling her ponytail around one finger. "It's like, a legend. Just pretend?"

"Yeah," Jake agreed. "Anyway,

Emmett stinks at art," he teased. "And neither of us had even heard of a golem until now."

"Umm, there's something else," Reisha said. "You wrote your name, *Emmett*, on its forehead in Hebrew."

"So?"

"Well, the Hebrew word *emet* means 'truth.' According to the story, that was the *exact same word* the rabbi of Prague wrote on his golem."

I froze. This was getting too weird.

"No way!" I exclaimed.

"Way. Right on his forehead. That's the actual word he used to give the golem life."

"Oooo, let's test it!" said Emily, who was now pulling her black hair up and twisting it behind her head into a scrunchy. Emily messed with her ponytail anytime she was excited.

"Definitely," Reisha nodded. "Emmett, this may sound gross," she said, "but I want you to gently blow in its nose."

"Uhhh, no way. I'm not going to get near that thing's nose. What if mud snot comes out?"

Jake giggled and puckered his lips. "It's your lucky day, Emmett. You get to kiss a golem!"

"Guys, I'm serious here. Don't kiss it. Just blow some air gently into its nose. It takes a quick puff of air to wake up a golem for the first time—at least, so the story goes."

I approached the mud figure. I turned my face sideways, drew in a breath, and puffed a short blast of air up its nostrils.

I stepped back. We all watched in silence.

Nothing happened.

Then, as if waking from a long sleep, the entire golem shook, raised its arms into a big stretch, threw back its head, and let out a silent yawn.

Wow, Reisha was right! My golem was alive.

CHAPTER 5

WE'RE OUTTA HERE!

The four of us made a pact: The golem would be our secret, and we would tell no one. Absolutely *no* adults could know.

We couldn't imagine what would happen if the grown-ups got wind of this. They would think we'd gone nuts and send us packing. Or they'd confiscate the golem and lock it away like they did with our phones. And that would be the end of that.

Jake, Reisha, Emily, and I were still in the woods with the freshly awakened golem. After its stretch and yawn, the golem stood still, just looking at us with blank eyes.

We had to figure out, and quickly: Could this thing be controlled? And how could we keep it under wraps at a camp full of nosy kids?

"Golem," Reisha commanded, "pick up that fallen tree over there." She pointed to a big dead maple trunk nearby. The golem headed straight for the dead tree, cradled its arms around the giant mass, and lifted it as if it were a toothpick.

I gasped. Emily's eyes widened. Jake stood with his mouth hanging open.

"Okay, golem, put it down please."

The golem dropped the tree trunk to the ground with a thud.

"That's incredible," Jake said. "How did it lift that? It's like five times its weight!"

"More like *sixty* times, actually," came a familiar voice from behind our backs. We whirled around to see Danny, comic book in hand, standing there with a huge grin on his face.

"Danny, what are you doing here?" I said.

"Saw you two headed out back and hiding something with a giant sheet, a sheet . . . white sheet . . . and figured you were up to no good. I was right," he said pointing at the golem. "Soooo, looks like we have a new bunkmate?"

We caught him up on what had happened, swearing him to secrecy, and Danny marveled at the golem's stunt with the tree. "Let's see, that tree probably weighs about 30 pounds per cubic foot, times about 50 feet long. That's at least 1,500 pounds, or like 680 kilos." Danny was a total whiz at math.

$$30 \times 50 = 1,500$$

"I'm guessing that's nothing to him, or her, or *it*," said Reisha, looking my creation up and down. "Well Emmett, you've outdone yourself this time."

"And you thought you were no good at art?" added Emily. "I'm ready to sign you up for art class for the rest of your life." My sis elbowed me in the belly, and I giggled.

"Well, if it can pick up a dead tree," continued Emily, her eyes widening, her hands flying up again to adjust her ponytail. "Just think! I mean, what we've got here is pure gold. Emmett, no one is *ever* going to even think of messing with you after they find out about this," she said, jerking her thumb at the golem. "And I have a few ideas about how to put our new friend to work this summer."

"Wait," I said, getting a little defensive. "This isn't your golem, Em. It's *my* golem."

"Yeah, but Reisha clued you in on waking it. As far as I'm concerned, Emmett Cohen, it is as much ours as yours."

This was typical Emily. What's mine

was hers. I had created this myself. Why did she think she deserved any rights over it?

"Okay, Danny, Jake—we're outta here! Grab the golem."

"All right, everyone, calm down," said Reisha. "Let's work together here."

The golem stretched its arms again and planted its legs on the ground, feet spread slightly apart. It looked like a soldier standing at attention, awaiting our next order.

"Golem," I commanded, "climb that tree." I pointed to the tallest tree nearby.

Without a second's pause, the golem leaped into the tree, arms arching widely to grab the next limb. It was already halfway up the trunk before Reisha yelled, "Golem, stop!"

And there it stopped.

"Golem, come down," she ordered. The golem instantly let go and thudded to the ground, facedown, barely missing Jake's head.

Jake laughed. "What an idiot!"

"Exactly. The golem is an idiot. It was just born, remember?'" Reisha said. "So we're going to have to teach it some things."

Reisha helped the golem back to its feet with a short command of "Golem, get up!"

There was a hole in the soft mud where it had landed.

47

"And we need to be really careful," said Danny. "This golem just climbed ten branches in five seconds. I counted. It can move at warp speed . . . warp speed."

"But how do we keep it from going haywire?" I asked. "Would it take commands from other kids too? I hope not."

"Well, if I recall the story correctly," said Reisha, "the golem stops if you erase the first letter, the *alef,* from its forehead. When that letter is gone, the two remaining letters spell the Hebrew word *meit*, which means 'dead.'"

א מ ת

מ ת

I shuddered. "I don't want to kill it," I said. "Just put it to sleep so it doesn't start

48

doing jumping jacks across our cabin in the middle of the night or backflips on the counselors' beds."

Jake and Danny snickered.

"Don't worry. You won't kill it," said Reisha. "You'll just put it to sleep. Try it."

I reached up and smudged the *alef*. Immediately, the golem went stone stiff and looked as it had earlier that morning.

"Whoa, that's so cool," I exclaimed.

I looked around and picked up a twig. Then I walked over to the golem and, using the twig as a pencil, etched an *alef* into its forehead. The golem yawned and came back to life.

That day, we swore ourselves to secrecy: No one—other kids, the counselors, and definitely *not* the Beetle—needed to know that there was an actual, real-life golem at camp.

CHAPTER 6

THE "MUD PACK" PACT

We created a secret, members-only society for the golem. It was Danny's idea. We called ourselves the "Mud Pack." The name sounded cheesy, but Danny insisted, and it stuck.

This society was desperately needed to keep the secret from spreading. But it was hard to keep this secret, as we soon found out.

Jake, for one, had trouble keeping his mouth shut.

"I'm so sorry, Emmett. Rob was talking about his baseball bat collection, and I just sort of let it slip," he shared one afternoon. "Dunno why it came up, but I just couldn't resist. I mean, it's Rob, okay—we tell him everything."

And before the second week of camp was over, Emily had blabbed to the twins.

So, what started out as a club of five— Jake, Reisha, Emily, Danny, and me— turned into a not-so-secret society of eight.

We called an emergency meeting of the Mud Pack. Everyone swore to keep their mouths shut, or else they would be left out of the fun. I half seriously told them that if they did blab, there would be an angry golem coming after them.

Danny had another idea too. "A secret society needs a secret meeting place. Like Batman and all the superheroes—they have secret lairs." Did I mention Danny knows everything about comics?

And who better to build one than the golem itself?

The woods behind the boys' cabins seemed like the perfect spot. There were plenty of trees and rocks to hide us from the prying eyes of our counselors and the Beetle. The counselors never really came back there anyway—which was actually kinda funny: counselors at a nature camp who didn't like exploring nature.

Lucky for us, Camp Teva is an awesome setup for hiding a golem.

The camp is split into two areas with clusters of cabins—one area for girls, the other for boys. In the middle of camp is the lake—just big enough for swimming and canoeing, and bordered on one side by woods that slope up a mountainside. A long path leads through the woods along the lake from the boys' side of camp to the girls' side.

On the opposite side of the lake is a clearing where the main camp buildings are located—the office, the indoor gym where we play basketball, the dining hall, and the B.K., short for *Beit Knesse*t, where we hold Shabbat services and camp assemblies and shows. Jake jokingly calls it "Burger King." The slanted roof almost makes it look like a fast-food restaurant if you turn your head a funny way.

Beyond that are the baseball field and the tennis courts boxed in with high chain-link fences. Aside from the gravel road leading into camp and a parking lot, we were surrounded by wilderness.

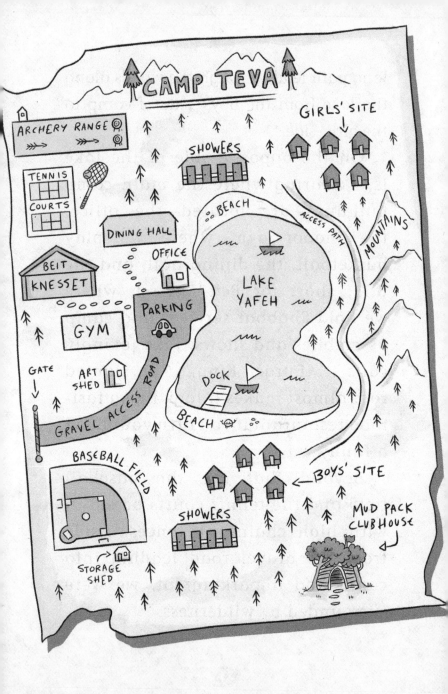

Very pretty, with lots of places to hide a golem.

Still, we needed to figure out a way to hide the golem in plain sight. Because we had plans for this golem.

One evening, Jake, Reisha, and I met up in the woods and "switched on" the golem to see if we could teach it some basic commands. I asked Reisha to join us, since she knew more about the legend than any of us and this knowledge might be useful.

The golem was a fast learner. It was a lot like training my dog, Silo, when he was a pup.

"Golem, hide!"

The golem stepped behind a tree.

"Golem, stand still!"

The golem stood frozen like a statue.

"Golem, be a rock."

The golem looked confused, then picked up a large rock.

"Perhaps you should demonstrate," said Reisha. "Show it what you mean."

I pointed at a large boulder on the ground. "Golem, make yourself into that shape, like this." I crouched down, wrapped my arms around my body, and tucked my head into my knees.

It worked! The golem dropped to its knees and curled its body into a tight ball. It was so tight that it looked like an oddly shaped rock.

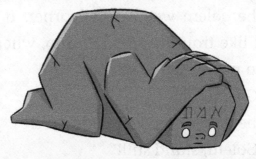

"Perfect. Golem, when I say, 'Be a rock,' I want you always to make that shape," I said. The golem's head peeled away from its balled-up body and nodded.

"Golem, back on your feet," I commanded. The golem lay tummy down and put its feet up against its back, like a pretzel.

"Hahaha!" Jake doubled over with laughter. "That's pathetic."

"No, golem—stand up with your feet on the ground," I commanded. This time the golem understood.

Jake smiled wide. "THIS is going to be one crazy summer," he said. Then he tried a command I hadn't thought of.

"Golem, speak!"

The golem's mouth started moving—its lips were rippling like waves on the lake—but no sound came out.

"Or not!" he said, smiling. "Thought I'd try that."

"Nope, don't think our golem can make conversation, Jake," Reisha said. "Okay, it's getting late. Let's put the golem to work and get back to our groups before someone notices we're missing."

"Golem," I ordered, "build a clubhouse. Use anything you can find—branches, leaves, stumps—and make it really big, so big that we could do jumping jacks inside. And don't stop until you've finished. When you're done, hide yourself inside."

"And if anyone comes near you, turn yourself into a rock," added Reisha.

The golem seemed to understand and started collecting branches. As we headed out to join our evening activities, I glanced over my shoulder, wondering if it was smart to keep a golem awake and working all by itself.

CHAPTER 7

A HUGE MESS

I woke the next morning when the sun was barely up and heard soft snores. I quietly roused the other Mud Pack boys from their beds, and we tiptoed out of the cabin without waking the counselors. I was excited to see if the golem had finished building our clubhouse—so excited, in fact, that the previous night I'd forgotten about my homesickness.

Expecting to find a neat little hut for our

meetings, we found that the golem had instead created . . . a *huge* mess.

Rocks, trees, and leaves were piled at least fifty feet high, and the massive mountain of forest debris looked as if it would topple over any minute. Branches were scattered everywhere.

The golem was still working and was about to push over a pine tree that was at least one hundred feet tall when it spied us coming. It immediately dropped to the ground and turned itself into a rock.

"Oh, *no!*" cried Jake.

"Golem, get up, and *stop*!" I commanded. It jumped up and froze in place.

Danny gazed up at the giant mass of branches. "Oh boy. That's definitely *not*, not what I had in mind when I said a *secret* lair. The counselors will see this mess a mile away."

The golem just stood there, blank-faced and awaiting its next order. "What a dummy," said Danny. "I mean, why why couldn't you have given it a scientist's brain . . . a brain . . . like the Hulk's?"

"Hmm. I guess my command 'so big that we could do jumping jacks inside' wasn't clear enough," I said.

"Well, in this case, the one who gave us this problem may also be the solution," Danny said. "Golem, can you please put these branches and rocks back where they came from?" Then he seemed to have a second thought. "And do it as fast as you can."

The golem snapped into action, moving so fast its legs were a blur. In less than fifteen minutes the pile of branches and rocks was nearly gone.

Once the golem finished that task, Danny drew a diagram of a clubhouse in the dirt. Jake and I explained that we needed a small house with a roof. "Like our cabin, over there, only smaller."

This time, the golem moved slowly and carefully, and as we watched and corrected, it soon built a proper clubhouse.

We stood back and admired the structure: tree branches stacked sideways to form four walls, supported by several tall trees. We hid the golem inside, erased the *alef*, and headed back to our cabin and to breakfast.

Later that day, the members of the Mud Pack returned during rest hour to find the golem still unmoving inside the clubhouse. We piled inside, pulled a large branch of leaves over the entrance, and held our first meeting.

Reisha had borrowed a whiteboard and some markers from the camp office, which she hoped Mr. Beetleman wouldn't miss. Jake rolled his eyes as she pulled out the board. "What, are we in school now?"

Reisha ignored him. "Okay, so we've learned a couple of things about this golem," she said, making a numbered list on the whiteboard:

What we've learned:

1. The golem is very strong. It can lift things many times its own weight.

2. It can move extremely fast or slow, depending on the commands it's given.

3. It's dumb as a rock but can learn to do tasks quickly.

4. It can remember commands such as, "Golem, be a rock."

5. It needs to be watched **AT ALL TIMES**.
It shouldn't be left alone.

6. It can be stopped by erasing the *aleph*.

"What we don't know," she continued, "is what else the golem is capable of. We'll need to test it some more."

"I have a question!" Emily cried out before flipping her head upside down to adjust her scrunchy. "Is this golem thingy a boy or a girl? You keep calling it an 'it,' but I think it should have a name."

"Oh, it's a boy, a boy!" exclaimed Danny. "You made it male . . . male—right, Emmett?"

"Who said it's male?" responded Reisha. "It's not human."

"Well, I think you're being sexist by saying it's male," said Emily. "As far as I'm concerned, this golem is a girl. Girrrrl power!" she yelled, pumping a fist in the air.

She was talking loud enough for the entire camp to hear. Everyone shushed her.

"I say Emmett decides," said Jake. "It's his creation. Emmett, boy or girl?"

I looked at my friends and shrugged. "I dunno. When I made it, I wasn't thinking about a boy or a girl. Just an ugly creature, nothing more."

"Okay, I have the answer," said Reisha. "Just so it's fair, this golem officially has no gender. It's not a boy or a girl; it's simply a golem."

With that decided, we started brainstorming a series of tests to help us understand what the golem was truly capable of, which would mean bringing it out of hiding and onto the camp grounds. Our plan was simple. We would lead the golem across the baseball field and over to the tennis courts, which were in a remote part of camp and were usually empty during rest hour. There we'd have more room for the golem's tests.

I was very nervous about being caught. I made everyone promise to walk in a tight group around the golem and to whisper the order "rock" if anyone came near us.

Not ten steps onto the field and there was the Beetle waving at us as we crossed the baseball diamond.

I was the first to spot him approaching. "Golem, rock!" I whispered. The golem crouched into position. Reisha, Emily, and Danny, who were at the back end of the group, nearly tripped as the golem collapsed in a heap.

"Hey kids, what's up?" asked the Beetle. "A little baseball during rest hour?"

"Umm, yeah . . . that's right! Baseball," stammered Danny, putting his hand up to his baseball hat. "We were just about to grab a bat and ball and some, er, gloves from the supply shed."

"What the heck is that?" Mr. Beetleman said, spying the rock that had miraculously sprouted up between second and third bases. "How did that boulder get out here?"

"Umm. Funny, we were just asking ourselves the same thing," said Emily, adjusting her ponytail. "It's crazy. It's like someone just dropped it here."

"Huh? People don't leave boulders in the middle of a baseball field," said the Beetle. He scrunched up his face, his forehead wrinkling. "Well, this just makes no sense. No sense at all. I'll see if I can get the maintenance team out here with a bulldozer or something to move it."

He scratched his head

and looked again at the rock. "It's just so . . . but how did it . . . ?" He continued mumbling to himself as he walked away.

We waited until he was out of sight before ordering the golem back up.

Our next stop was the tennis courts.

The courts were at the far end of camp. As expected, they were completely deserted.

Time was tight, so we started the tests right away.

"Golem, jump as high as you can."

The golem crouched down and leaped up high into the air, like a gymnast but without a running start.

"Whoa," said Danny, "that was at least ten feet from just standing in place."

"Golem, let's race!"

Jake, being one of the fastest kids, challenged the golem to race to the other side of the clay courts, crossing about eight courts to the end of the fenced-in rectangle and back. Jake and the golem lined up, we gave instructions, and Reisha yelled, "GO!"

The golem shot out like a race car and was gone in a cloud of dust before Jake had even taken his first few steps. In less than half a minute the golem screeched to a halt right where it had started.

Jake just threw his hands up in the air. He was still at the opposite end.

"Oh my goodness," said Emily. "That golem just put one of the fastest kids at camp to shame."

"That was exactly 21.3 seconds," said Danny, checking his digital watch.

"Hmm, I wonder," said Jake. He grabbed a few tennis balls and a racket.

Jake demonstrated how to hit a ball over the net. He handed the golem a racket and jogged around to the other side of the court. "Okay, golem, return this." The golem walked around the net and handed the racket right back to him.

"No, that's not what I meant," said Jake. "You stand on that side and hit the ball over, like this." He demonstrated, hitting a ball with his racket across the court.

This time, the golem hit it right back.

Then Jake fired a bunch of balls at

the golem all at once. Some were well over its head. Regardless of how high or fast, the golem returned every single one, zigzagging back and forth across the court at lightning speed. Then it swung too hard and there was a ball-sized hole in its racket.

"I counted forty-eight balls returned," said Danny, glancing down at his watch, "in exactly two minutes and fifty-five seconds."

Next, Emily demonstrated a cartwheel, then ordered the golem to imitate her. The golem went head over heels again and again. Before she could yell the command for it to stop, the golem reached the end of the court and crashed through the fence, toppling headfirst down a short cliff and into a dry creek bed. It landed with a thud at the muddy bottom.

Danny was cracking up. "Fifteen cartwheels and one fence taken down."

"Oh no, golem, come back!" commanded Emily. "And fix the fence." The golem cartwheeled back up the hill and started pulling the fence together, without much success.

On our way back to the clubhouse, we stopped at a wooded spot near the lake. "I wonder if our golem can swim," said Reisha.

"I'll bet it's like an Olympic swimmer!"

I responded. "Golem, jump in and swim."

The golem approached the lake but stopped just short of the water's edge.

"Golem, swim!" I commanded. The thing wouldn't move. We tried to nudge it forward, but nothing worked. For some reason it seemed terrified of the water.

CHAPTER 8

MAKING A LIST

The next day at Mud Pack HQ, I drew up on the whiteboard a list of potential tasks for the golem.

We debated lots of ideas. Here's what the list looked like:

Golem To-Do List

#1: Whip up some food or steal some treats from the dining hall.

#2: Get our phones out of the locker in the camp office.

#3: Help with cabin cleanup chores like sweeping the floor, making beds, and cleaning the bathrooms.

#4: Disguised as a camper, help us win some games on our softball team.

#5: Build a zip line for camp.

#6: Help stop global warming.

We liked all these ideas but ruled a few out right away. There was just no way I was going to put the golem in a softball game disguised as a camper. It was too risky. Building a zip line, which our camp lacked, was way too complicated, and I doubted our golem was smart enough to do it safely.

Rescuing our phones was out of the question too. Too dangerous. The golem might be caught, and that would be that.

Reisha had added number 6. She wanted to use the golem for good—to plant trees, rescue birds, scare off lumberjacks, that sort of thing. Nice idea, but again too risky, and reluctantly we crossed it off the list.

Which left numbers 1 and 3. I had my own ideas too. But those didn't make the whiteboard—I kept them in my head. I didn't want the other kids to know that I missed my dog, Silo, so much that I had considered sending the golem home to bring my labradoodle to live in the clubhouse.

We were now three weeks into camp. Thinking about Silo made me feel homesick. Sometimes I cried a little at night before falling asleep. I missed playing tug-of-war with Silo over his slimy old chew toy. I missed my dad's slightly burnt mac 'n' cheese. And I missed my room and my own bed.

I didn't tell anyone, but I even considered having the golem pick me up and run me home after dark, just for the night. That was impossible, of course, but it had crossed my mind.

One afternoon during lunch, while Jake and I picked at our chicken lo mein, Jake suddenly looked up. "We need some real food," he said. "Tonight we put the golem to work."

I nodded in agreement. We both had had enough of the gross food in the dining hall.

That evening, as soon as it was lights-out, Rob quietly snuck out the back and headed to the clubhouse. He read the golem a series of commands. The Mud Pack had all agreed on the task, and we had written the exact instructions down on a piece of paper.

About an hour later, at around eleven o'clock, our deliveries silently arrived. Jake heard the golem's clunky footsteps on the stairs and grabbed a flashlight. He opened the door to find a large cardboard box on the landing.

On the girls' side of camp across the lake, Reisha and Emily opened their cabin doors to find a similar unmarked cardboard box.

We opened our boxes to find our reward. Ice cream! Bottles of chocolate syrup! Cans of whipped cream! Danny's eyes lit up as he quickly took stock. "Six pints of ice cream—chocolate, vanilla, strawberry—two bottles of syrup, three cans of whipped cream," he whispered excitedly.

The golem had crashed the dining hall on our orders. It had broken the kitchen locks and run off with the camp's ice-cream supplies.

At night after lights-out, the counselors liked to leave our cabin and hang out on picnic tables near the camp office. As long as we were quiet as mice, we could do as we pleased inside our bunk.

We quietly woke the other boys. Using flashlights, we constructed a sundae assembly line. Jake and I even made little paper hats to make it look like we worked in an old-fashioned ice-cream parlor.

The other kids in our cabin were amazed. "Where did you get all this?" someone asked. Jake played dumb. I made up some story about bribing a girl on the kitchen staff. The other kids were too busy loading up bowls with ice cream to give it much thought. Some had seconds, even thirds. I guess we were all kinda hungry from not eating the flavorless lo mein dinner earlier.

The next morning at breakfast, none of us was particularly hungry, the ice cream still filling our bellies. Mr. Beetleman stood near the kitchen with a group of counselors.

Reisha, who was sitting nearby, overheard their conversation and had to put her hand over her mouth to stop herself from giggling.

"This lock is broken," said the Beetle, pointing at the kitchen door. "And look here, there's mud smudged on the lock."

"And there are mud footprints on the floor," added Miss Rachel. "Someone tracked mud everywhere."

"Look at those footprints—they go from the freezer to the cabinet and back," said the cook. "The ice cream is almost all gone. Whoever did this knew exactly what they were after."

The Beetle hustled out of the dining hall. "Why isn't anyone eating breakfast today?" he mumbled as he passed our table. I looked over at Jake and Rob with a knowing smile.

That afternoon, we returned to our cabins to discover that our little feast from the previous night had attracted some unwanted guests.

Ants were swarming over a bowl in one corner of the cabin and under some of our beds. Mice had crawled through the floorboards to eat chunks of paper from the empty bowls. Ice-cream droppings had turned our cabin floor into a sticky mess. It felt like someone had put double-sided tape on the floor, our shoes making a "schlepp, schlepp" sound with every step.

Our counselors put two and two together and called a group meeting.

"Okay, guys, what happened last night?" asked Benjy.

We all just stared. I tried my best to imitate the golem—stone-faced and trying not to crack a smile.

Jake couldn't help himself and started laughing into his hand. He wasn't laughing for very long. Our counselor handed him a bucket and a mop and told him to get busy.

I later heard from Emily that a similar scene had played out on the other side of camp. An emergency meeting was called, and the girls were assembled and interrogated about how they had gotten the ice cream. Lilly and Rebecca denied everything until someone ran into the cabin and brought out two sets of bright-yellow matching pajamas—obviously the twins'—which were sticky with globs of dried chocolate ice cream.

It was Friday, so that evening we all put on white clothes to welcome the start of Shabbat, the day of rest. We gathered for services at the B.K. and listened patiently as Reisha led the camp in Hebrew songs and prayers, flawlessly of course. After the short service, Mr. Beetleman took the stage to make announcements, as he always does. But this time he looked concerned.

"I'm very sorry to say we have an ice-cream thief at camp."

After a lecture about Jewish values and telling the truth, he reminded us that since someone had eaten all the ice cream, the rest of the camp would have to go without until supplies were restocked. Some of the kids groaned.

A few shot angry looks over at us.

But those kids were no longer angry when they saw what was for breakfast the next morning.

Part two of Jake's food plan was for the golem to turn into a chef and make us a real breakfast instead of the usual hard-boiled eggs, toast, and cereal. For this, Jake had managed to swipe a cookbook from the shelf in the kitchen when the cook's back was turned.

Overnight, the golem had gone to work on our orders. Following instructions we had read to it from the cookbook, the golem had created a huge feast: chocolate chip pancakes, challah French toast, freshly made bagels with cream

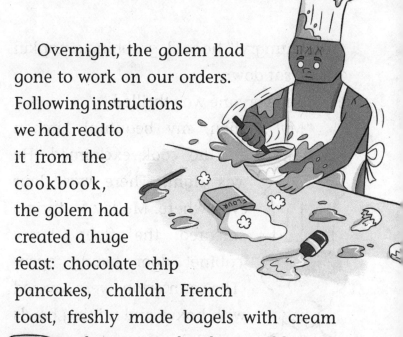

cheese, and cheesy blintzes. Freshly squeezed orange juice. Fresh donuts. The works. Our feast was neatly laid out on every table in the dining hall.

Kids whooped with joy. Some just stood with their mouths hanging open. "This is the best day ever!" I heard one of the younger kids gasp. Jake just took it all in with a wide smile. "Boy, am I hungry!" he said, grabbing a napkin as he sat down.

Not everyone was thrilled.

"My kitchen, my beautiful kitchen is destroyed," the cook exclaimed. He was right. There was flour everywhere. Muddy footprints smeared the floor. Every cabinet door swung open. The countertops were covered with boxes and mixing bowls and batter-coated spoons. There were grease puddles on the stove.

"Shoot," whispered Jake. "We forgot to give the golem a 'clean up' command."

The Beetle looked more confused than ever.

"Who could have done all this?" he muttered in between bites of pancakes and syrup. "Mmm . . . that's good," he added, licking his lips, and then grumbled, "The lock on the kitchen door is broken—again! After I just had it fixed . . . Oh, these blintzes."

"It's as if a catering company came in overnight and took over," said Miss Rachel. "I just don't get it. But these blueberry muffins are *sooo good*," she said, exhaling, tucking a napkin into her shirt collar and diving into the feast.

As the other adults and kitchen staff huddled, voices low, trying to solve the mystery, we enjoyed the greatest feast of the summer.

CHAPTER 9

ATTACK OF THE CAMP CRITTERS

The mess was one thing we hadn't thought about when we ordered the golem to bring ice cream and cook breakfast. It was as if we had sent out party invitations to every Catskills critter, big and small.

Stomachs still full from our glorious breakfast meal, we returned to our cabins to find that squirrels and mice had invaded. "I guess we didn't do a very good job cleaning up yesterday," Rob said, pulling a paper bowl covered with ants from under his bunk.

Other animals were on the prowl too. A black bear was seen lurking near the dining hall. Chipmunks were sniffing around our doors.

Reisha's cabin had been infested by several battalions of angry-looking ants.

Our counselor Benjy turned the job wheel on our cabin wall that morning, and I watched as "Emmett" lined up with the chore of taking the trash out to the dumpster. Which meant touching the ants. Yuck.

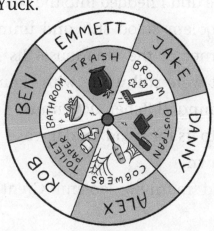

But there was more.

"Okay, kids, when we get back to the cabin after lunch, we are going to have to do a really good job cleaning up this cabin," said Benjy, "and that means washing the floors and making sure there are no more sweets lying around. Yesterday, I found a squirrel looking for treats in my shoe."

With the thought of having to do a deep clean hanging over our day, it was time to put the golem back into action—on cleanup duty (number 3 on the whiteboard list)! Jake and I headed into the woods.

The golem stood stiff and unmoving in a corner of the clubhouse. Its hands and feet were still white with flour from the morning's kitchen adventure. I added the *alef* to its forehead, and it woke with a giant yawn.

"Good morning, golem! Great work

with breakfast," Jake cooed. The golem smiled, then lifted its hand to meet his. We had taught our golem how to make a "high five." That was its newest trick (Jake's idea, naturally).

"Okay, golem, your job today is to help us clean up our cabins." Jake pointed to the critter-infested cabins on a map he had drawn on the whiteboard. "Wash and polish the floors, and wipe down anything that's sticky."

"And, if you see or hear anyone coming, hide," I added. "Do this as quickly as you can. Start working only after everyone has left the cabins for activities. That's at 9:30."

The golem nodded. After leaving it with a bucket of cleaning supplies we had gathered from a camp supply closet, we headed to the campgrounds for morning activities.

Benjy was first to open the door as we arrived back to our cabin a couple of hours later. I was carrying a large, three-legged stool I had just finished sanding in woodshop and couldn't grab the door handle.

"Whaaaat happened!!!" said Benjy. "This place looks and smells amazing! Kids, was all this your doing?"

The beds were made, the shelves organized. The toilets and sinks in the bathroom sparkled. Our clothes were neatly folded and stashed away. It looked cleaner than the day we first arrived.

Too clean, actually.

The floors were so clean they shimmered. The golem had gone a tad crazy with the floor polish and had buffed

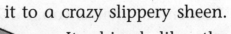

it to a crazy slippery sheen. It shined like the slick wood lanes of a bowling alley.

Benjy took one step in . . . and slipped . . . and slid . . . and tripped across the floor. He landed in a heap at the far end of the cabin.

Danny followed. He took one step, slipped, slipped again, and slid, then fell on his behind with a loud THWACK.

I carefully stepped inside. It was like an ice rink, except in summertime. We took off our shoes and skated across the floor in our socks.

After Danny and Benjy recovered from their spills, they got up and joined in too.

Later that afternoon we were surprised at the all-camp assembly when Mr.

Beetleman invited cabin 15 to come to the front of the pavilion. That was us! We looked at each other nervously, then stood up and shuffled our way forward.

"Well, wonders never cease," he said. "What was once one of the messiest bunks in Camp Teva history is now the cleanest. Campers, I'm pleasantly surprised to announce that this week's award for the 'Cleanest Bunk' goes to the boys in cabin 15!"

The entire camp cheered as we waved from the stage and accepted our Cleanest Bunk ribbons from the Beetle. Benjy was so proud. "You beat everyone," he yelled as he gave all of us fist bumps and started to sing "We Are the Champions"!

Somewhere in the back woods, I'm sure the golem was smiling.

CHAPTER 10

GOLEM = TROUBLE

Dear Mom and Dad,

Hi from camp! So far, things are pretty great. Hard to believe we've been here four weeks already. Guess what? I lost one of my bottom molars yesterday. It was so gross and it bled! I did a monster march around the cabin and scared everyone with my bloody mouth. Hahaha!

I signed up for art, just like you asked. I'm also doing archery, swim lessons, baseball, and canoeing. In art, I made a funny statue out of mud, but I'm not sure it was all that good. Guess what else? I'm not as homesick this year! And I made a new friend. His name is Danny. He's really good at math, and he loves comic books just like me.

Please give Silo a hug from me!

Emily says "Hi."

Love, your favorite son,
    Emmett

PS: Have you heard of a golem? Reisha told me a story about it, and I'm wondering if it's true, or just made-up.

The summer flew by from July to August. Between cookouts, hiking trips, activities, and sports, everyone at Camp Teva was having a blast.

No one had found out our secret. But that was about to change—big-time.

It was my fault. Tempted by the golem's powers, I got lazy. Danny added up what happened in mathematical terms:
Temptation + Laziness + Golem = Trouble.

It was a ninety-five-degree day—dry and hotter than a desert—and I had left my towel at the tennis courts. After a long day playing in the stifling heat and the long walk back to my cabin, I was drained. It was my favorite towel too—the Philadelphia Flyers. The thought of walking back to retrieve it from the far side of camp was too much.

"The golem!" I thought. I walked into the woods and woke it with a scratch on the forehead. I gave it clear instructions to find my towel while staying hidden in the woods, and off it went.

The golem's stealth was impressive. It found a way to cross the camp without being discovered. But just as it reached for my towel, it was spotted.

Some six-year-olds still believe in monsters. So when Gabe, one of the smallest and youngest kids at camp, saw the golem reaching for my towel, he screamed at the top of his lungs.

The golem dropped into "rock" mode, but it was too late. The

kid came tearing across camp, hollering about a monster on the courts. Mr. Beetleman jumped out of his office chair and grabbed a few staff to join him. They started a camp-wide hunt, thinking there was an intruder on the grounds.

Jake was walking back from the lake and was the first to hear the panic. He grabbed me, and we rushed over to the tennis courts. We quickly moved the golem into the woods, ran back to our cabin, and prayed things would fix themselves.

For a hot minute, things did settle down. But that wasn't the end of our problems. As it turned out, little Gabe had been in the art shed when I made the golem. He thought he *recognized* the monster he saw on the tennis courts and told this to some of the adults.

Miss Rachel stopped by our cabin.

"Hi, Emmett! Haven't seen you at the

art shed in a while," she said. "I've missed you, buddy."

"Hi, Miss Rachel. Yeah, I just got busy with all the other activities. I might take art again before summer's out."

"Oh great!" she said. "By the way, whatever happened to that clay statue you made that first week of camp?"

Here was a question I hadn't prepared for. I felt my face turn red.

"Umm, it was kinda scary and so, I . . . umm, I took it out to the woods and threw it into the creek and it kinda, umm, dissolved. So, yeah, that's what happened!"

"Hmm. That's a shame. You worked so hard on that project. Well, oddly enough, one of the little campers thought they just saw something similar to it walking on the tennis courts," said Miss Rachel. "You and your friends wouldn't try to pull a prank on the little kids and dress up like your monster, would you?"

"Oh, I'm not much into pranks," I said as seriously as I could. "Jake is, for sure, but he wouldn't try and scare the little kids. Are you sure that kid wasn't imagining it?"

Miss Rachel paused. She seemed to consider the idea that Gabe had imagined the monster. "Yeah, I guess you might be right. Gabe is such a dreamy kid, always wandering around camp and getting himself lost," she said. "I'll talk to his counselor, see if we can calm him down."

But the strange happenings at camp were beginning to pile up.

The following afternoon we were at an all-camp assembly. We were all seated quietly, facing the stage and listening to a counselor talk about the kinds of birds you might see and hear on the nature trails. Suddenly, from the middle of the pavilion came the unnatural sound of a cell phone ringing.

Mr. Beetleman, who had just started to ask a question about the Eastern wood-pewee, stopped cold. "What was *that*? Who has a cell phone?"

Silence. The phone continued to *brrring*! It was an old-fashioned phone ringtone.

"Okay, kids, we have one hard-and-fast rule at camp. No cell phones, no exceptions. If my ears aren't playing tricks on me, someone may be breaking that rule. I hope that's not the case."

Silence. The Beetle finished asking his bird question. Moments later, a different ringtone sounded from a different part of the B.K.

The Beetle stopped mid-sentence again.

A third phone sounded from the front row.

"Well, this is getting ridiculous! Okay, kids, I'm going to ask everyone who has a cell phone in their pocket to please stand up. Now!"

Reisha shot up from her seat, looking slightly embarrassed.

I gawked at her. She turned a burning shade of red and mouthed, "I'm sorry."

A moment's pause. Next stood Emily. Then Jake. Then the twins in hard-to-miss, floral-pink print dresses.

Then it dawned on me. *The golem had freed their phones!*

Later, back at the clubhouse, the twins couldn't stop laughing.

"It was all Emily's idea!" said Lilly.

"That was so awesome," added Rebecca. "I texted all my friends back home. Wait, Em, how did you get them?"

"Why don't you ask the golem?" Emily smiled.

"I can't believe you. You sent the golem?" I stammered, my anger rising.

"What happened to the Mud Pack rules? We agreed that no one would use the golem without a vote. We should use him to help all of us, not just some."

"Oh, yes, Emmett, do tell us all about that rule. Mister 'I-left-my-towel-at-the-tennis-courts!'"

"Okay, okay, I said I was sorry. But we have to be careful. The Beetle is getting suspicious. You want us to get caught?"

"No, of course not," said Emily. "I just . . . needed my phone. I never finished texting my new friend that I wouldn't be home all summer. I didn't want her to think I was ignoring her."

Just then Emily's left hip pocket rang.

"O-M-G, really!" I yelled. "You were supposed to turn that back in."

CHAPTER 11

A COMPLETE MESS

Emmett:

Thanks soooo much for your letter!
We're so pleased you tried art!!!
Please remember to be nice to all
the kids in your bunk and include
everyone when you play together.
Silo misses you, but he's happy and
spending most of his time playing
ball and chasing his tail.

You asked about a golem: Those
stories are made-up nonsense.
There's no such thing as walking
clay statues! Tell Reisha to stop
trying to frighten you.
I never told you this, but dad's
family has some connection to one
of the rabbis in Prague who came
up with that legend. I'll check
with Pappy the next time we talk.

Lots of love, xoxo!
　　Mom

The heat wave that started the day I lost
my towel dragged on for nearly a week.
When the heat finally broke, the sudden
temperature drop brought a forecast
of severe thunderstorms and hurricane-
force winds. The staff was worried and
decided the safest place at camp was the

gym where we play basketball. It was the strongest building at camp, made of cinder block and a reinforced steel roof.

The plan was for us to sleep there overnight until the storm passed. Over the next few hours, the camp staff worked to move our sleeping bags into the gym. Mr. Beetleman and the office staff were busy answering phone calls from worried parents, assuring them we'd be safe.

Reisha was concerned about the golem, and so was I. "It's going to be a bad storm. It might not be safe in the clubhouse," she said. "The rain could damage the golem."

"Yeah," said Danny. "No wonder it's afraid of swimming. Just think: rain plus golem equals . . . mud!"

"Guys, we can't walk the golem into the gym with us," I said. "Miss Rachel thinks I destroyed it. Besides, they said only sleeping bags, flashlights, and a book are allowed—nothing bigger. The golem will just have to ride out the storm in our cabin."

Before nightfall, Jake and I snuck back into the woods and woke the golem. We walked it nearly all the way to our cabin. We were about to erase the *alef* when the Beetle himself appeared, coming around a path on the other side of the cabin.

The golem immediately dropped into rock mode.

Thankfully, the Beetle hadn't noticed. He was busy looking up at the sky. "Rain's coming soon. Oh, hi, kids!"

"Heyyy there, Beetle, er, Mr. Beetleman," stammered Jake. "We're just getting ready to head on over to the gym."

"Good idea! I'll come with you. But first, gotta rest these tired feet for a minute." He walked over to us, took one look at the golem-rock and . . . *sat down right on top of it!*

"Ahhh . . . So this storm that's coming– let me explain to you how it formed. . . ."

I saw his mouth moving. But to this day I couldn't tell you one word the Beetle said.

He was sitting *right on top* of our golem. Smack in the middle of camp.

I looked over at Jake nervously. His eyes widened. I prayed the golem would keep still.

While Mr. Beetleman talked, I nervously shifted my weight from foot to foot and tried my hardest to keep a straight face and not panic.

Suddenly Mr. Beetleman stood up.

"What the . . . ? Did that rock just move?" My heart skipped a beat.

He looked at the "rock" under him. "Nah, I must be going crazy. This storm is making me loopy. Come to think of it, this entire summer is making me nuts. Rocks growing out of the ground where no rocks were before. A breakfast feast out of thin air. Missing ice cream. Critters in cabins. Cell phones popping up everywhere. Kids, my head is spinning!"

He walked off, looking slightly dazed. Jake and I let out a huge sigh of relief.

That night, as the wind whipped around the gym and thunder shook the walls, all I could think of was our poor golem alone in the cabin. What if a tree fell on the roof or water came through the walls and soaked it through? What if a bolt of lightning set the cabin on fire?

Around midnight, we heard the first tree crash to the ground outside. I mentally prepared for the worst. The golem might be a lost cause.

None of us slept much. We heard the wind howling, jumped with every tree falling, felt the thunder shaking the earth. Danny was lying in his sleeping bag next to mine near a foul line on the basketball court. He was counting the seconds between the lightning flashes and thunder.

"One Mississippi, two Mississippi, three Mississippi, four Mississippi, five." CRACK. "Okay, that means the lightning strike is about one mile away."

The following morning, we stumbled outside to see just how bad the storm had been.

Trees were down everywhere. Some had fallen on cabins. The art shed was completely smashed by a giant oak tree that had split in half.

"At least that's no big loss for you," joked Jake. "But Emily and the twins are going to be a wreck at that sight."

Then, more bad news. The entire camp was cut off from the outside world. Huge oaks had fallen onto the main road leading out of camp, making it impossible to pass. Phone lines were down. Electricity was cut off. So was cell phone service. A complete mess.

Jake and I ran back to our cabin. The golem was standing in its corner, unharmed and untouched. "Phew. The golem's safe."

We looked at each other, and in that brief moment, we both smiled.

"Jake! Are you thinking what I'm thinking?"

"I think so. Yep. How terrified we were the first time it smiled and winked at us, right? I almost wet my pants."

"Actually, that's not what I was thinking," I said. "I was thinking about how quickly the golem cleaned up that mess it made out in the woods. You think it could do that trick again, but on a slightly bigger scale?"

"Oh wow! Great idea!" said Jake. "Let's call the Pack together."

An hour later the entire Mud Pack assembled in the woods. The clubhouse luckily had survived the storm.

Lilly and Rebecca were in tears. "The art shed is lost, and I had so many good projects in there," said Rebecca.

"That's the least of our concerns. I just heard the Beetle say the entire camp might have to shut down because of all the damage from the storm," said Reisha. "This could be the end of the summer for us all."

I stepped to the whiteboard. "Boys, girls—and golem—I think I have the answer."

As the sun set that night, out of the darkness of the woods emerged a hulking shadow. It lurked until the last flashlights dimmed in the cabins. Then it set to work.

CHAPTER 12

CAMP IS RESTORED

On a normal day, the entire camp wakes up to the sound of a scratchy recording of a bugle playing on a battered old record player in the main office. The bugle's song was piped across camp through a series of horn speakers mounted on trees.

Some camp traditions are weird.

That morning was different. There was no wake-up call. The sound system had been damaged in the storm.

I woke up with my stomach grumbling. The previous night we had to make do with snacks instead of dinner, because the kitchen was still not up and running.

Jake, Danny, and I stepped outside. We were nearly run down by the Beetle.

"Kids—Emmett! Danny! Jake! Reisha told me everything. But how did you do it?"

"Do what?" I asked, just before he grabbed the three of us in his arms and pulled us into a giant group hug.

I figured the game was over. Reisha had blabbed, and he'd found out about the golem.

"Everything's fixed!! The cabins repaired, the trees removed. It's a miracle! I've never seen a group of more resourceful, thoughtful kids in my life."

"Umm, what exactly *did* she tell you?" I stammered.

"About all the work you kids did to fix

the camp last night," he said excitedly. "At first when I saw the trees removed, I thought Sullivan County had sent a cleanup crew. But then she explained how you sawed the trees by hand and moved them in pieces. I can't believe it. It's like I'm in a dream. Oh, wait." He pinched himself.

"I guess I *am* awake. This is too real to be a dream, right?"

"I'm pretty sure this is not a dream," said Jake, smiling broadly. "And yes, we did it all ourselves. It was all of us. I used the saws from the woodshop. Rob moved those fallen trees with his bare hands. And Danny and Emmett, well, they can do just about anything with a hammer and nails."

The Beetle just smiled and shook his head in amazement. He bought the whole crazy story!

We headed off to breakfast, amazed

at the golem's success at fixing camp. Fallen trees were sawed into pieces. Logs and branches were stacked neatly on the side of the paths. Damaged buildings had been repaired.

The art shed looked about as good as new—if you looked at it while standing on your head.

"Oh, no!" Reisha exclaimed. "This is all my fault. I told the golem to rebuild the art shed 'from the ground up.'"

It was something to see. The slanted roof of the art shed was on the ground, the door hanging wide open to the sky, the floor now a roof. Other campers just stood and stared at the upside-down building.

"Umm, I guess we need to fix this, Mr. Beetleman," said Reisha. "It's hard to rebuild things at night, when it's so dark in the woods."

Mr. Beetleman was in disbelief. I looked over to see him slapping his face with both hands.

"Well, I'm gobsmacked," he muttered to himself. "How did those kids do all this? Am I awake? I need some coffee. Hmm, actually, maybe I should drink less of the camp canteen coffee. It's bad enough as it is."

CHAPTER 13

GOLEM TO THE RESCUE, AGAIN!

Camp was winding down. Parents would be arriving in two days to pick up their sunburned and worn-out "happy kiddos." Which created a huge problem—because we still couldn't agree on what to do with the golem.

The golem was too large to fit into a car. And Miss Rachel thought I'd destroyed it. That thing couldn't suddenly make an appearance on the last day of camp. Then the Beetle *would* lose his mind.

Could we hide it in the woods? Too dangerous. What would happen if it accidentally came to life or was discovered by a hiker or a hunter or something like that?

The Mud Pack held a meeting. We knew the golem had to stay at camp. But we needed to hide it somewhere it couldn't be found—and with its powers neutralized.

We came up with a plan. We would wipe the Hebrew lettering entirely from its forehead to be extra safe and then hide it in the old storage attic above the camp pavilion.

We were trying to figure out how to move it there when suddenly there was a piercing alarm over the loudspeakers. We all tumbled out of the clubhouse to find out what had happened.

It was the camp's special alert system for a missing camper. The police were called, and everyone divided up and started searching the camp and the woods nearby. In this case, little dreamy Gabe, that six-year-old kid who was so frightened after seeing the golem on the tennis courts, had gone missing.

I was afraid one of the adults would stumble on the golem during the search, so Jake and I headed for the clubhouse to turn the golem into a rock.

We arrived at the clubhouse to find . . .

It was gone.

I stared at the empty corner. "Where's the golem?"

We quickly rounded up the other members of the Mud Pack again and checked to see if anyone had seen the golem or given it instructions. Everyone insisted they hadn't. So we started our own frantic search party.

"Are you sure no one sent it on an errand?" asked Emily, eyeing us suspiciously as she twisted her ponytail into a knot.

"No!" I replied. "Last time I saw it, it was standing right there in the corner. I even removed the *alef* myself."

We all started running across camp, frantically trying to find both Gabe and the golem.

A minute later Rob cried out, "There it is! . . . I mean, there *they* are!"

We were on the wooded path that led

to the lake. And there in front of us, rising from the water, was the golem, holding in its arms a scared-looking and sopping-wet Gabe. Behind them on the lake was an upside-down canoe.

We rushed over as the golem carefully placed Gabe on the beach.

Gabe was too shocked to speak. He took one look at the thing that had saved him, his eyes grew huge, and he fainted.

Emily and Reisha ran over to wake up Gabe and help him back to his feet. Then they started walking him down the path back to the cabins.

I looked at the golem's forehead. The *alef* was still smudged, just as I had left it in the woods!

Just then the golem's knees buckled.

Actually, they just collapsed. And its legs started to fall apart.

So did the rest of its body. The golem's clay body was literally falling away in hunks.

"It's the water!" cried Jake. "It's making the mud dissolve."

I dropped to my knees and started to try to push the runny clay back into place. But the mud was too squishy and just slid back to the ground. "*Nooo*," I wailed, "please, don't go."

The golem was crumbling to pieces.

Within minutes, there was nothing left of the golem but a pile of shapeless clay.

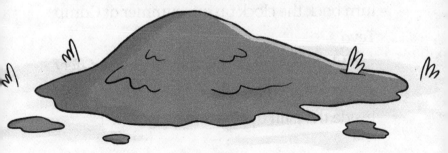

CHAPTER 14

THE GOLEM'S SACRIFICE

Our cabins were bare. The beds stripped down to the mattresses. Our belongings were packed and waiting outside for our parents' arrival. The summer was over.

Not even the strength of a golem could turn back the clock on our summer at Camp Teva.

What was left of my art project was safely stored in an empty plastic bin we had found inside the (still upside-down!) art shed.

I told the Mud Pack I was pretty sure I could rebuild the golem, but there wasn't time, with camp closing. We stored its muddy remains in the bin, and Rob, Jake, and I hoisted the box up the steep stairs leading to the attic over the B.K. pavilion. There we hid it under some canvas tarps.

"Are you sure you got all the mud into the bin?" asked Jake.

"As much as I could scrape off the ground," I said. "I think there's just enough to re-create it next summer. I'm pretty sure it was something in the special mud from the art shed that helped to bring our golem to life. We'll need to keep the lid tight so the mud stays damp."

How the golem rescued Gabe remains a mystery. None of us had given it orders. And the *alef* was smudged from its forehead, which should have kept the golem in a frozen state.

Reisha had a theory. "In cases of extreme danger, a golem could possibly have the power to come to life on its own," she told us at the final meeting of the Mud Pack. "My guess is the golem sensed danger and woke itself. Let's face it, that's what golems are supposed to do. They're there to help people in trouble."

"Wow, so it's not as stupid as we thought?" asked Danny. "Like it *sensed* danger, and its 'Spidey-senses' tingled."

"Our golem is a real hero," said Emily.

"Remember the time it wouldn't go into the water at the lake? This time it did go into water, maybe even knowing that it wouldn't survive," added Reisha. "It made the ultimate sacrifice to save that boy."

I felt a lump in my throat and had a sudden impulse to run back to find the golem and give it a big hug. But then I thought twice. I'd feel pretty dumb hugging a shapeless mound of clay. And I'd have to explain to my parents why I was coming home from camp in clothes smeared with mud.

"Well, this just stinks," said Lilly. "I just had the best summer of my life, and I can't tell anyone why."

"Yeah," sighed Rebecca. "Our friends would think we'd gone bananas."

We all laughed. Who would believe we'd spent our summer with a golem?

Later that afternoon, Jake and I were sitting on our packed-up trunks when our parents pulled their cars up to the cabin. We ran out and gave them big hugs and kisses.

We lifted our things into the cars, and I said my final goodbyes to Jake, Rob, and Danny.

"Emmett, remember you are *not* allowed to make another golem at home," Jake reminded me. "Only when the Mud Pack is together again. You have taken a sworn oath—remember that, bud."

"I swear, no golems. I'll stick to stick figures and squiggly rainbows."

As my parents pulled the minivan out of camp, Mr. Beetleman was at the main gate to say farewell and hand back our cell phones.

"Goodbye, Emmett and Emily, the two Ems. We will miss you! I'm sure you'll fill your parents in on all the crazy things that happened this summer and how you saved the entire camp."

"Okay, Mr. Beetleman, we will. Goodbye."

"So long, kiddos."

"What was that all about?" my dad asked. "Saved the camp? I know there was a storm, but what does he mean?"

"Oh, nothing. The Beetle's had a long summer. I think he drank too much of the camp 'Beetlejuice' or something," I joked.

"I wonder what he does in the off-season," said Emily. "Do beetles hibernate in winter?"

Mom and Dad laughed. "Good one, Emily!"

"So, Emmett, tell us about art. Did you like it?" asked my mom.

"Brilliant," I said. "I loved art. I think I'm going to take it every summer from now on. I hate to admit you were right, Mom, but art class was pretty cool."

I winked at Emily. She grinned and pressed the power button on the side of her phone. The screen blazed to life.

And with that we headed home to Philadelphia.

While Emily happily texted away, I dreamed about next summer. Maybe our golem could build a giant water slide. It might collect fruit from the tallest trees, install TVs in the cabins, or play a monster in the camp show. Or maybe getting that thing to stop global warming wasn't so crazy after all.

If you had a golem at your camp, what would you have it do?

THE END

Hey Reisha, ru home yet?

Reisha

Emmett! Yep, I'm back home! 😃 You?

Yep. I was googling about golems the whole way home. CRAZY stuff

Reisha

No kidding. I'm in the library right now

I found this old dusty book with a leather cover

It says it's really hard to make a golem. The person who does it has to be like a super-rabbi or something. "Pure, clean, and close to God"

That's def NOT me

Reisha

Yeah, did you even shower more than once the entire summer? Doubt it 😅

ROFL

What else did you find out?

Reisha

Remember when you blew in the golem's nose to wake it up? There are other ways to bring golems to life too

U mean I didn't actually have to do that?

Reisha

The book says u can write the word "God" on a piece of paper and put it in the G's mouth to wake it up

Whoa! 😵 Good to know for next time

I read that some rabbi like 400 years ago went into the attic of the Old-New Synagogue in Prague and came out shivering and pale

He made them seal the door so no one could go up there

Reisha

No way! That's where the first golem was made. Maybe it was still there

I'm glad our G wasn't big and scary like that one

Reisha

It HAD to be scary. That was the point!

The original golem was made to protect the Jewish villagers from angry mobs

Wait, is this a true story or a legend?

Reisha

The mobs really happened. Who knows if the golem was real

Reisha

WE do! 😃

Ha! See ya 👋

TODD GUTNICK spent many of his early summers as a camper, then counselor and head counselor, at an overnight camp in Massachusetts. When he's not writing for fun, he is the Senior Director of Communications at the Anti-Defamation League. A native of Pittsburgh, Pennsylvania, he lives in South Orange, New Jersey. This is his first book.

RUTH BENNETT is an illustrator and animator. She studied animation at Norwich University of the Arts in England, and she lives in a small country village in the heart of Norfolk, England.